HARVEST
OF
SKULLS

GLOBAL AFRICAN VOICES

Dominic Thomas, *editor*

Abdourahman A. Waberi

HARVEST
OF
SKULLS

TRANSLATED BY
DOMINIC THOMAS

Indiana University Press

BLOOMINGTON & INDIANAPOLIS

This book is a publication of

Indiana University Press
Office of Scholarly Publishing
Herman B Wells Library 350
1320 East 10th Street
Bloomington, Indiana 47405 USA

iupress.indiana.edu

Published in French as *Moisson de crânes: textes pour le Rwanda* © Abdourahman A. Waberi. Paris: Le Serpent à Plumes, 2000. Published by arrangement with Agence littéraire Astier-Pécher.

The paper used in this publication meets the minimum requirements of the American National Standard for Information Sciences—Permanence of Paper for Printed Library Materials, ANSI Z39.48-1992.

Manufactured in the
United States of America

Library of Congress
Cataloging-in-Publication Data

Names: Waberi, Abdourahman
A., author. | Thomas, Dominic
Richard David, translator.
Title: Harvest of skulls /
Abdourahman A. Waberi ;
Translated by Dominic Thomas.
Other titles: Moisson de crânes. English
Description: Bloomington : Indiana
University Press, 2016. | Series:
Global African voices
Identifiers: LCCN 2016017816 (print) |
LCCN 2016020660 (ebook) | ISBN
9780253024329 (pbk. : alk. paper) |
ISBN 9780253024411 (ebook)
Subjects: LCSH: Genocide—Rwanda. |
Rwanda—Ethnic relations. |
Tutsi (African people)—Crimes
against—Rwanda. | Hutu
(African people)—Rwanda.
Classification: LCC DT450.435 .W3313
2016 (print) | LCC DT450.435
(ebook) | DDC 967.57104/31—dc23
LC record available at
https://lccn.loc.gov/2016017816

1 2 3 4 5   21 20 19 18 17 16

Contents

Hear this, you elders;
give ear, all inhabitants of the land!
Has such a thing happened in your days,
or in the days of your fathers?
Tell your children of it,
and let your children tell their children,
and their children to another generation.

JOEL 1:2–3

Preface: Postgenocide Rwanda

One almost feels like opening with an apology for the very existence of this work. The process of writing itself was somewhat grueling, repeatedly deferred over weeks and even months. Were it not for the moral duty owed to various Rwandan and African friends, these words may not have risen to the surface quite as expeditiously as they did following two trips to the Land of a Thousand Hills.

Nonetheless, when it comes to my own modest personal journey, bereft of any political activism, no human experience has thus far proved as challenging, urgent, or demanding. This explains my fervent desire to simply vanish, to be forgotten, to refrain from adding to the general pessimism, for it to be my turn to play dead. This book makes no claim to explain anything whatsoever, and the leading role is given to fiction. The imagination and subjectivity are there merely to nourish the book's nervous system.

"Genocide: the term is overused. I reserve it for the Holocaust and maybe a few other cases," the Jewish-American linguist Noam Chomsky informs us. He is someone who knows a few things about linguistic subtleties and controversies. The Rwandan genocide was the first to be recognized by the community of nations since 1948. I wonder who the next anthropologist will be to come along and remind us that societies are built on shared crimes?

Adorno's famous dictum on "the impossibility of writing after Auschwitz" was always there in the back of my mind, deep in my unconscious, or at least I assume so, but so too was the brutal statement by the German-language poet born in Romania, Paul Celan: "Only one thing remained reachable, close and secure amid all losses: language." The power that language has garnered in our chaotic world is so alarming—and not only in these Africas mired in lawlessness, stricken at these times with a deficit of hope—that we need to recognize the need to pay close attention, or at the very least to maintain a healthy distance, from this language.

How many bodies are we talking about? Falling, stumbling, caught by the ends of the hair, finished off, emasculated, defiled, raped, incinerated? How many? In each and every crisis, language remains inadequate in accounting for the world and all its turpitudes; words can never be more than unstable crutches, staggering along. More often than not, under different skies, this same language remains a luxury that is beyond the reach of most people. And yet, if we want to hold on to a glimmer of hope in the world, the only miraculous weapons we have at our disposal are these same clumsy supports. What else can we do except remember those souls and beings who have perished, concentrate on what they have to say, gently touch them, caress them with awkward words and silences, glide over them because we can no longer share their fate? If we feel up to the task and if they are willing to take part, one may even find a way to make them smile a little. Say out loud the names of all these people poisoned early on, of all the lessons tarnished by hate and the selfishness handed down. Turn oneself into a chamber of echoes. Erect a pantheon of ink and paper dedicated to all the victims; call on those consciences willing to listen. Revisit the history of this country set on a path to self-destruction or, more accurately, ushered along in its demise by a long-standing criminal regime. What more can be done? Maybe one should just lay low. Maintain silence around us and lend an attentive ear. Summon up our patience as well. And, with a little luck, you might be able to stand in as a crucible for the stories and testimonies of survivors. Having said this, expect discouragement at every corner, both ahead of and following each and every encounter. We persist in saying that the role of literature, this maker of illusion, with its willing suspension of disbelief, remains negligible. Or ask ourselves how fiction can remedy this situation. In our globalized world, journalistic accounts aren't any more useful, gnawed away as they are by indifference, admittedly well-informed yet reluctant to respond expeditiously or effectively. And finally, one may well ask, what gives us the right to speak in the first place? And with what authority? And let us not forget that the machete was not the only instrument available to the torturer: the writings and sheer symbolic power of several Hutu intellectuals, such as the historian Ferdinand Nahima or the linguist Léon Mugesera, to name just a few, were mobilized toward the final solution. One catches oneself daydreaming after a long bout of depression and disillusionment. Trying to convince oneself that what was undone yesterday by the death-dealing power of the pen can today be healed over by the same pen—or at the very least, we are not prohibited from giving it a try.

When Wole Soyinka recently appropriated the now-infamous statement "A single death is a tragedy, a million deaths a statistic," he did so as a deliberate provocation. The nature of our humanity calls on us to give, if only momentarily, a face, a name, a voice, and, leaving, a living memory to the hundreds of thousands of victims so that they don't end up as mere numbers. Or worse even, stored away in the vault of memory or at best abandoned dormant in the columns of a spreadsheet more or less officially recognized by our so-called collective conscience, one that must be regularly strengthened, more often than not hurriedly and intermittently—hardly recommended in terms of effectiveness. We should avoid at all costs expecting Rwanda to stand in the eyes of humanity as a permanent reproach of our negligence.

"My memory has a belt of corpses," Aimé Césaire wrote in *The Notebook of a Return to a Native Land*. Following the Martinican poet's example, let us weave memories so that the denialists, who either have no qualms about speaking openly or seek instead anonymity on the internet, don't show up to weed, definitively this time, all the graves and the cemeteries. Let's try and reawaken, restore even, that part of humanity that was lost in this country. Let's set on paper the long story of these infamies. Let's start writing.

The Sunny Side of Life*

Recently one evening, as trails of ochre tinged with mauve kept stretching late into the sky of Mantua, I found myself face-to-face with Predrag Matvejević, the writer from Mostar and host of the writers' conference. He was alone with a bottle of red wine, looking grim. The man who had gone all over the now-defunct Yugoslavia seemed to carry the disappearance of a part of the world on his slumped shoulders. In a moment of extremely lucid weariness, he said to me: "It's your turn now!"

That way of passing on the role of witness from Europeans to Africans would have seemed like melodramatic posturing were it not for the feeling of urgency I sensed in Predrag Matvejević's gestures and voice. No, there was no hinting at the African Renaissance advocated by ex-president Thabo Mbeki, nor was it an act of redemption supposed to atone for who-knows-what by taking the formerly colonized people back to the sunny side of life. I politely turned down the large glass of wine he offered me and disappeared into the night of Mantua, or more exactly, went off to join some colleagues whose conversation was livelier: they were arguing endlessly a few tables down, happy as birds in paradise. Hours later, the words of the melancholic author of *Mediterranean Breviary* were still trotting through my head. I had to track down in the African sky the flame of hope close to Walter Benjamin's heart, or at least find a few reasons why the future should belong to the people of Africa. To do this, it doesn't help to follow the present state of the continent in a press that delights in the disasters of the day. The fate of the African continent is always distorted by the words of others, caught in their dreams, and seen through their commiserating and secretly frightened eyes. You can picture it galloping alone toward the abyss. And the facts do their best to justify them. Indeed, a large part of the continent, from the Horn of Africa to Mauritania, from the Gulf of Guinea to Zimbabwe through the area of the Great Lakes, is sliding into the empire of misery. Since the end of the Cold War, new types of warfare have appeared, grafted onto old motifs (rebellion, stealing of resources, irredentism, etc.) or been newly invented (like the pirates along the Somali coast). And these conflicts are far less comprehensible than the previous ones.

What would be the point of remaking the recent history of this continent, of pitting one view against another? Let's rather slip inside what looks like a possible opening, stand inside the zone between reality and imagination, the only place that can be fertile when enriched with knowledge and ideas. Africans, like everyone else, show the same poignant, pitiful stubbornness we all do in dreaming our lives, in wrapping them up in words. Like old Job, the writers of Africa will never stop shouting at the world. They can never be quiet or laze away in the bright sun of righteousness.

Rwanda, Fifteen Years Later

A small country the size of a postage stamp, densely populated, farmed and managed for centuries by a native monarchy, Rwanda had been spared predatory slavery—always synonymous with cultural bleeding. Even if colonization was a terrible breakdown of their civilization, the Rwandan people still have the talent and care to deal with the business of running a country. Nothing like the disorder, the artistic creativity, of their neighbors who sing, dance, and waste their energy in cathartic libations.

Nearly fifteen years after the Tutsi genocide, it is still very difficult for foreign observers and the international community to follow the development of this country with a neutral eye and without being prejudiced or excessively emotional. Some try hard to denounce the postgenocide Rwandan government, despite the fact that legislative elections have just been organized for the second time and took place peacefully. Rwanda goes its own way, without taking into account the advice of the international community, for which it doesn't have much regard anyway. And rightly so. Others emphasize the impressive achievements that have been made since 1994. Stopping the genocide and bringing the country back from Dante's inferno is not the least of the feats for which we can credit the former guerrillas of the RPF, the Rwandan Patriotic Front. They have now swapped their battle dress for respectable-looking suits and ties.

Stephen Kinzer, a former *New York Times* journalist and recognized biographer, belongs to the second group of foreign observers. He recently published the first biography of the man who presides over Rwanda's destiny: Paul Kagame. The task is daunting. Kagame and his comrades-in-arms were the stage directors of a world soaked in misery and apparently bereft of any hope. Somehow they fashioned a Rwanda that has been returned to all its children, available to winners and losers, exiled and survivors alike. The velvety curves of the Rwandan hills echo with the songs of children and the shouts of farmers, some of them former prisoners released from jail by the Gacaca courts. Although Stephen Kinzer is passionate about his subject, he can keep his distance, nonetheless, according to his own criteria at least: his involvement and passion don't prevent him from being accurate and precise. He knows how to use the details that will give his subject the aura of myth. Well documented and strengthened by thirty interviews with the former little refugee turned president, the book is also enjoyable.

When you close this book, you won't be able to say that Rwanda is an abandoned corner for the dead. You'll learn that it is a country standing tall on its thousand hills, set back into orbit, ready for life and economic recovery. The past won't be like a rearview mirror acting as a constant reminder of guilt, nor will it stand in front of you like a tyrannical master. The past is with you, very close to you, not to be forgotten, as the new Kigali Genocide Memorial suggests.

How can a dispassionate, efficient political system be established without going through a majority elected to the detriment of a minority, creating a permanent climate of hostility between two antagonistic political camps? Rwandans have to come up with the answer to that question. The solution for now is to be found in a fine balance between the main party (President Kagame's RPF), and six other small ones. The representatives of three "vulnerable" groups must be added to the mix: women, the disabled, and young people. In a country where the words "majority" and "minority" are charged with deadly connotations, such a heterogeneous but original coalition deserves praise for even existing. Not everyone is pleased with this motley crew, obviously. Many are critical of it, particularly among its opponents from abroad, from Belgium in particular, who accuse the RPF and its leader of nipping in the bud any dissonant voice, and Human Rights Watch is certainly right about stressing the complete lack of opposition in this newly elected house.

Houses, roads, and avenues are as fleeting, alas, as the years. This is the thought borrowed from Proust that's in my head when I arrive back in Kigali. I don't recognize anything, almost nothing, in the city I walked through for two months in 1998 and 1999. It's true that memories sometimes have their own recipe for reinventing the reality that created them, but this city could not be more different from the one I visited nine years ago. Completely transformed, and also thriving. Malls everywhere, roads, homes right out of an American suburb. The dream has no limits for someone who knows how to combine energy and integrity. A wind of renewal is blowing hard and the good news spreads like wildfire in business circles abroad. Kigali is about to become the meeting place for philanthropists and decision makers: they all compete with each other to come up with the most daring project. Bill Gates pulled a lot of money out of his pocket to stop the spread of AIDS; Bill Clinton is a frequent visitor to this country, which has often been praised by the International Monetary Fund (IMF) and the World Bank as a model country. Tony Blair offered his services as a sherpa to President Kagame, said to be his personal friend. According to a *Wall Street Journal* study, Rwanda, in 2006, was the frontrunner in Africa in the fight against poverty. Now that Rwanda is secure, the government concentrates on the economy and the social sphere; the impulse moves from the bottom up: in 2003, parity was implemented, giving women access to the highest positions in politics. By establishing equality between men and women, Rwanda has pulled itself up to the very top. A real feat in a country where tradition didn't tolerate women expressing their opinions publicly. No wonder, then, that Kigali looks amorously at the big bankers and patrons of the Anglo-Saxon world, like Blair, Gates, and Clinton!

Standing atop the Gisoir hill, the Kigali Memorial, completed in 2006 with the help of a British NGO, is the newest thing in the spotlight. The basement is filled with huge vaults containing 250,000 corpses, all people killed in the Kigali area. On the first level, there is a terraced garden designed around large funerary plaques, as well as several exhibition halls—you can feel here the American touch and even detect a kind of family resemblance to the United States Holocaust Memorial Museum in Washington, D.C. The permanent exhibit manages to combine the concern to educate the public about the 1994 genocide with the will to open up to other genocides (the Holocaust, Armenia, and Cambodia), while focusing on testimonies and the individual identities of the deceased. Finally, the sponsors of the memorial did not forget to point a finger at the UN, at the former colonial powers, and particularly at the tortuous meanders of French politics.

The Forgotten People of Bisesero

But things are not perfect, far from it. For instance, the country's reconstruction has bypassed the survivors, who are part of a mostly silent minority. It isn't that there is any political will to marginalize them, but the result of the economic policy carried out by the political elite (many of whom came back from exile after 1994) has been the further deepening of existing inequalities. And thus, the survivors are more vulnerable and are hit harder by the problems other Rwandans have to face. You can't find, for instance, a single road sign on the twenty-mile trail linking Kibuye, the capital of the Western Province, to the Bisesero hills, where Tutsi farmers hunted by the perpetrators of the genocide resisted heroically. The government is eerily absent. The Bisesero museum is empty and its attendant nowhere to be seen, on that day at least. The survivors and their children come out of their shacks, extremely surprised to see foreigners. Nobody comes to visit, they say. The angry howling of the wind against the eucalyptus trees. Throughout our visit, many show signs of impatience, and seem mentally fragile too. Some were taken to Arusha to testify before the ICTR, the International Criminal Tribunal for Rwanda. With the risk of reopening the wounds that have not yet healed. Then back to square one. Forgotten right away again. As if their long shepherd's crooks and their coats, too large for their skinny bodies, had made no impression on the NGOs swarming all around the big cities. Nor did the survivors receive the benediction of the American churches whose representatives traipse around the rest of the country.

Yet the last general census of July 2008, which completed the data of the 1998 census, shows that part of the present administration wishes to acknowledge these problems and hopes to alleviate the fate of the 309,368 survivors.

Constructing the Memory of the Genocide

A tug-of-war between the French government and those who oppose its politics and its "francophone strategy"[1] is rare, even

unique, in the annals of African history. The roots of this ada-
mant resistance are to be found partly in the genocide, as the
damning Mucyo report[2] shows us. Divorcing France to marry
America is indeed ironic: to be overtly americanophile is now
the new elite's dogma.

Whatever the shortcomings of this government, which has
its own political agenda and does not always treat its outcasts
well, this is a nation truly committed to remembering its genocide, even in dealing with its internal problems.[3] This includes
reviving traditional, often subversive cultural practices: black
humor in songs and theater, the ironic use of choreographic
figures in the traditional *intore* dance, the feudal art of the drum
now appropriated by women. Constructing the memory of the
genocide also includes an unprecedented outpouring of writing. Besides the books written or the films made by foreigners
or Rwandans who have come out in France and Belgium, col-
lecting texts at the national level is also important; conducted
by associations of student survivors (AERG), such work sometimes leads to writing workshops at the University of Butare.

A New African World War?

Between 1998 and 2003, "the first world war of Africa," as a
high-ranking officer of the U.S. State Department termed it at
the time, saw eight armies fighting and led to between four and
five million deaths in the former Zaire. There was a real risk
of its spreading throughout central and southern Africa, from
Angola to Tanzania, from Chad to South Africa.

Since the end of October 2008, Joseph Kabila's troops
(FARDC), supported by various paramilitary militias, have
been fighting the deposed General Laurent Nkunda, a Congolese Tutsi, with the help of Rwanda. Nkunda claims to be
fighting to protect the Congolese Tutsi minority (to which he

belongs) from the Hutu militias who have been active in the eastern region of the Democratic Republic of the Congo (DRC) since the end of the Rwandan genocide, but as Kigali is trying to establish a safety zone on Rwanda's western side, we have reasons to be wary. Laurent Nkunda accuses the Kinshasa regime of discriminating against his ethnic minority, the Tutsis, and threatens to overthrow Joseph Kabila, whom he claims is backed by Angola.

The power struggles with ethnic overtones are not the only reasons for war, of course. North Kivu Province has important mining resources; gold, tin, and coltan are much coveted and greed is highly conducive to flare ups. Such is life, with both great achievements and challenges, in Rwanda and in the region of the African Great Lakes.

I should add just a few words. The title of the main short story that follows, "Terminus," comes from the Latin word *exterminare*, which means "to drive out, expel, banish." This is the origin of the French word *exterminer*, in other words "to annihilate down the last one."

Acknowledgments

Special thanks are due to Nocky Djedanoum and Maïmouna Coulibaly (from the organization Fest'Africa) for their moral and technical support, to Gratien Uwisabye and Théogène Karabayinga for introducing me to Rwandan society and for being such dependable and friendly guides. Warm thanks also to Dr. Rufuku for several in-depth discussions, to Clément-Robert Rutemderi for his somewhat erratic yet helpful insights, as well as to Benjamin Sehene and my good friend Sofiane, who, like so many of his compatriots in exile, transited via Djibouti. I owe a particular debt of gratitude to all the people in Kigali and elsewhere in Rwanda and Burundi who so generously gave their time and often also their hearts. And finally, of course—it could hardly be otherwise—this book is dedicated to the memory of the victims of the genocide.

HARVEST
OF
SKULLS

FICTIONS

TERMINUS

Until very recently, when they were replaced by various synthetic materials, violin strings were traditionally made from animal tendons, called gut strings, usually from a cow or a horse. The harmonious and the sublime, it would therefore seem, can be extracted from pain and suffering. Does the same hold true for the Achilles tendons of Tutsis, so hideously severed from living beings shortly before they were massacred? Might they be susceptible to producing tropical symphonies as a tribute to close relatives or folks from here and elsewhere, to the various family clans living up in the hills, to the loamy soil coating the fertile terraced hillsides, to the rain, the lush vegetation, and the streak of lightning splitting the skies? Are there two kinds of people, just like there are two kinds of tendons, those who are fundamentally good and those who are inherently bad? Those who console humanity, like the conductor and violinist Yehudi Menuhin, and others who are mere flesh eaters?

The script is pretty much the same everywhere. The local civilian population gathers in an administrative building, usually in a school or a church, in response to an official announcement made by the mayor of the municipality or on the national radio. Then, a triage process is carried out, separating longtime neighbors, parishioners, childhood friends, inhabitants of the same compound. Hutus are asked to vacate the premises immediately. Grenades are tossed haphazardly into the assembly. Machine guns open fire. The Rwandan house is given a thorough cleaning. And then, finally, the hell of the *Interrahamwe* (those that attack together) militia and their machetes. Humans writhing, contorting, emptying of their substance, twisting like an earthworm chopped in half.

Kinyarwanda is a language that now has several unique terms, such as *itsembatsemba* (extermination) and *itsembabwoko* (genocide). These previously unknown or unprecedented terms will henceforth have a place in the language for eternity.

Independence Day was celebrated on July 1, 1962, on what was apparently a rainy Sunday. Already there was talk of the threat represented by exiled Tutsis and of their blind allegiance to the monarchy, plans for a secular peace were being stonewalled, and the sowing of the seeds of future discord was under way. Already people fantasized about genocide—the word as much as the deed. The small territory was on the verge of suffocation. A new slogan became fashionable: "Work will set you free." In the air and in people's minds, a languid and casual sense of anticipation, of pending violence, was tangible. People covertly hoped for incandescence and conflagration. Of course, the pogroms would soon follow.

The Hunting Season Is Open

Children born into the wrong families are rounded up and locked away in dark cells, forced to share a space with vermin, rat poison, and pesticide. They gradually succumb to pleurisy, starvation, and a slew of other unspeakable hazards. Quietly, laboratory tests are carried out. Quite freely, in the light of day, the violence begins, uninterrupted from that point on. No inquiring eyes—not a single reporter or observer—will come from the outside. No wonder: it is the beginning of a new era and people are full of euphoria at the end of the Cold War, Asia is thriving, Africa has the wind in its sails, the social revolution is in full swing in the postage-stamp-size country, whereas right next door, the imposing, conquering Mobutu belches from wealth and boredom, busy dictating the list of his desires to the cowardly deadbeats of this world.

The exiled, vivaciously amassed on the perimeter of the motherland, breathing in her unique fragrance, live in sub-human conditions—hopeless young people enlist for distant campaigns, as far afield as Mozambique. They hold on to the grittiness of their mother tongue. After all, Lilliput in exile must learn to bide its time or else come up against its older brothers with the help of Belgians, the French, the Americans, the Catholics, the peasants, the Protestants, and the apostles of development. The helpful and the enjoyable work hand in hand, as do the subjective and the passionate.

It is not the head of a civilization that
begins to rot first. It is the heart.

AIMÉ CÉSAIRE
Discourse on Colonialism

Rue de la Serpette, Nyamirambo

A small flat bottle of *uganda waragi*, a type of whiskey made in Uganda, sticks out of the back pocket of his olive-green battle dress, a walkie-talkie hangs from his waist, and the young RPF officer, much like all his comrades hanging around, seems as calm as Buddha. The walkie-talkie crackles and after some static sound orders can be heard. As for the soldier, he can see clearly and into the distance at night; this is a question of habit, but given the escalating mayhem and lunacy also a matter of life and death for a rebel watchman like him. The missionaries of powerlessness, humanitarian organizations, and the NGOs often arrived long after the harvest, like flies swarming a butcher's block.

Those with the privilege of having skulls have been around for a long time. The world is divided into two separate camps, and not only because of having a skull above the shoulders. Skull bearers are equally archaic in terms of what they have to say and the way they move, and this has been the case ever since the forgotten ancestor *Homo erectus* first stood upright not far from here, in the Great Rift Valley, to be precise. Now extinct, they no longer realize just how old-fashioned they have become. Pouring gallons of ink into the local newspapers won't change a thing for them. Henceforth, we have entered a period of infamy, gone beyond the fable; the presidential jet has engulfed the world. Only survivors are left to complain. Us . . . the world of fluids . . . obfuscated as with an abruption of the placenta, an impossible parturition. . . . We allow people to say, lead them to believe, that it was only a partial eclipse:

Killed . . . I killed him with my own hands . . .
Yes: a fecund and copious death . . .
it was night. We crawled through the sugarcane.
The cutlasses were chortling at the stars,
but we didn't care about the stars.
The cane slashed our faces with streams of green blades
we crawled cutlass in fist . . .

AIMÉ CÉSAIRE
And the Dogs Were Silent

Harvest of Skulls, Continued

Giggling and trumpeting prisoners a stone's throw from the scene of their crimes. To set forth and bring to the light of day their activities is an impossible task. Criminals all think they are completely innocent. When questioned, the response comes in a weary voice and impersonal manner: "We weren't there when the crime occurred!" Calamities are best when not shared. We are just poor peasants. We didn't see it coming. Hear anything. The folks in town might know something, those who headed out in big cars filled with machetes and plastic gas cans. We're just waiting for the rain to come, for a sign from heaven to start the seeding. We had a good life here before, the Tutsis lived up in the hills just like everyone else, we worked well together. We didn't see it coming. We couldn't do anything. We were worried they would kill us too. You can't revive the dead. They seemed to be saying that either no one was to blame or that everyone was at fault. Our lips are sealed, just like they were yesterday. Even when censorship is not handed down, society finds a way to get organized and impose its own prohibitions.

World, beware, there is a beautiful country
that they have spoiled with dissolute
unreasonable larvae a world shattered
flowers dirtied with old posters
a house of broken tiles of leaves torn apart without a tempest.

AIMÉ CÉSAIRE
And the Dogs Were Silent

Small country of escarpments, hills, valleys, and lakes, today transformed into a land of sorrow and ossuaries. It remained relatively calm over time, isolated in its mountainous fortress; things gathered momentum around 1959 or so. Misfortune skips and dances on the arm of History. The hills, enveloped in thick darkness, are invaded by bovine militias pushing their way through the entangled stalks, proliferation of branches and the climbing vines. Preparations for a harvest of skulls are under way. A theater that rots away the eyes and the mind, when one has not already completely lost it, that is. People are rallying behind the rumors, plunging us into the fermented sludge. He who remains silent consents. A cathedral of blood and ash emerges—a cathedral worthy of the thousand existing parishes in the small country or those of our friends in the Vatican. A magnetic cathedral that attracts fugitives and traitors, like the Sainte-Famille Church left in the capable hands of Father Wenceslas Munyeshyaka.[1] In the meantime, no ripples, dead calm, the UN couldn't give a damn; faced with warmongers, Kofi Annan merely shrugs. Oh well! We weren't waiting for the Messiah or a miracle maker! There's nothing to see here, move along! And yet . . .

Shipments of gleaming machetes, purchased cheaply in China, are arriving every day at Kanombe airport. We start unloading them, promising the cockroaches unprecedented levels of violence. All the while chugging bottles of Mützig beer and Cuban rum. Shirtless, mopping the sweat from our faces and listening to Simon Bikindi's patriotic songs aimed exclusively at the cultivators' receptive hearts, before reloading the shipments onto trucks ready to crisscross the seven hills of the capital for distribution in the various neighborhoods. Placed under the banner of chiefs with brows furrowed from permanent anger, we gnawed away at our nails waiting to be unleashed on those two-headed serpents, those lepers to be banished forever. All men and women bearing frail necks, including unborn children, are tracked without respite. They don't stand a chance. Let's be honest, not beat about the bush: they're screwed, done for. In the land of the Bible, they're made, like sheep, worse than rejects. Even crushed or dismembered, we can't be sure they're dead, so we go back over the bodies and finish them off with anything we can lay our hands on, a machete, a scythe, a club, a bludgeon, a Kalash, a sickle, an axe, a stone, a big stick, a tree trunk, an iron bar, a bayonet, a shank, a stake, a bullet, a rifle stock, burning tires, a brick. We chanted on the way home. They won't have the luxury of heading back to Ethiopia along the Nyabarongo River, we won't give them time for that. The scoundrels will be completely exterminated. Never again will we hear stories about yesterday, of bygone days, or of tomorrow. Never again will we have to listen to someone spinning a yarn that opens with the naïve or arrogant words "Once upon a time." Never again will someone utter the instructions "Touch me here, now my head, my chest, my stomach. Where's my head? My body?" Why is there so much emptiness around me? The only eye contact that remains will be with a deep sky, second to none. The maps of taste, pain, and remorse have become indistinguishable. Try as we may to escape the killings, they continue to haunt us. We made a covenant with the cleansing fires from the depths. It's dark and cold all around us. The city was completely surrounded, the cockroaches were armed, and we were afraid of their gunfire. A plot had been hatched against our people, the powder keg was ready, all that was left was to ignite the match. We had to fight back, outrun the lightning, set up a rear base for the women, the children, and the disabled. This was our Inquisition Tribunal! The name of the last blockade escapes me now, the number of infiltrators. I only killed three puppies, a trifle, that's all. It's coming back to me, now I remember, it was down at the Christus Centre, in Remera. You could hear the enthusiastic patriotic voices of Kantano Habimana and Valérie Bemeriki on the radio. O Bene Sebahinzi, the sons of the father of the cultivators, come to my rescue. No regrets, no tears. Not in our house. It's as easy as can be. The floodgates had opened, a gust of madness sent by the Devil to set us on that abject path. I don't feel well, I'm ashamed to mention it even, perhaps you can understand. I have some kind of an intestinal problem and am spewing thick white pus. I am the fury of the unchained soil. I'm going to end up like my brother Jean-Bosco, or like the other one, Paterne, who's now blind.

of the dead circulating in the veins of the earth
who at times come and break their heads against the walls
and the screams of revolt never heard
which turn in tune with musical tones

AIMÉ CÉSAIRE
Solar Throat Slashed

Mark is our seasoned guide for the genocide site, but in reality he's not that old himself. He lets us know how the skies are inclement, how there has been a shortage of rain in recent years. Now there is a drought and the runoff water from the bursts of rainfall destroys everything in its path. People are very unhappy about this. Dead bodies keep turning up in the papyrus reeds, the wells, after a bush fire, when the land is tilled ahead of seeding or after a torrent of water has come cascading down a steep hillside. Not a day goes by without someone finding a wrapped mummy, abandoned without burial by nameless killers. They sauntered in one day in the way animals do and just killed everyone; only my youngest, the girl over there who is now old enough to draw water, escaped, thanks to Divine Providence . . .

And the bloodshed continues in Kanyarwanda.

JOSEPH NSENGIMANA
Tous pour la nation

THE CAVALCADE

Just imagine what our green and unspoiled hills looked like in the early days of creation, long before the filthy cattle arrived, long before the meager lyrical song of the crossbow, the long-legged women with their high headdresses descended in small groups from the barren and incandescent Abyssinian plateaus. Even then they carried with them the diseases of the dry lands. Imagine, brothers of the hoe, the look of terror and bewilderment in the eyes of these brave farmers when the cavalcade of hordes appeared, the warriors leading the way, women and clusters of children following the herd. A torrential stream, an impetuous current, a genuine deluge as in the story of Noah's Ark. Without place, gods, or fire, the nomads ransacked, killed, scorched the earth and the people on their way through. The nomads—perhaps your memory needs refreshing, my children—arrived on foot, forced to abandon their horses earlier up north because of the thickness of our protective forest. They brought enslaved captives along with them to use as servants, interpreters, or sorcerers. They seduced us with their woven white cotton fabric from Ethiopia. We were treated worse than cow dung. Our fathers' fathers were the ones who learned how to show deference and loyalty to the masters of the earth and the seas. They learned how to die with them and for them in silence. At sundown, they never forgot to stoke the fire with fresh peat. Eyeless, they hovered in the way children do around their masters and the herd. They knew their place exactly; one cannot be in two places at once. Harmony and peace, that's how things used to be. God was happy on this earth, but we weren't. For centuries, that's the way things were. That's how the world was transmitted to us orally, but henceforth, with the help of the Most High and all our sons and daughters, a few adjustments will need to be made, by any means necessary. A car starts to sputter when the motor is ailing, and the mechanic has to get his hands dirty in the oil and grease. Nothing has changed in this regard since biblical times. Didn't the Romans teach others how to use torture as a political weapon in order to safeguard the general interest? I'm sure you won't disagree that the secular wisdom of our fathers has its limits, and that our future depends on us responding to the new challenges that come with modern existence. Marriage outside of one's ethnic group must be prohibited. This makes perfect sense and is in accordance with the Scriptures and in keeping with the guidelines promulgated by our social revolution. Likewise, civil servants, even outside of committed relationships or marriage, may not be distracted by their devilish women, whose forefathers came across the Red Sea and turned our agricultural paradise into this valley of tears. I can see from your reaction that you think I'm exaggerating—go ahead and seek advice from our friends the White Fathers, dive back into your Bible, but it might be more straightforward to take a closer look at the evidence. If you knew how to take the country's pulse you wouldn't hesitate to agree with me now, would you? Here you are, take this as an example. We are blamed for just about everything. The mutilated nose of Queen Hatshepsut's Sphinx, that's us. The drought in East Africa, us again. Sleep sickness, still us. Everyone spins the rough wool of oblivion when it comes to us, becoming more blind even than he who cannot see. Be strong, assertive, be good, and show no mercy. Our own situation is so special that we have no need for stimulants as they do elsewhere in Africa; our only drug is hatred. May God preserve you from the doubt and hesitation so dear to skeptics and to those other two-headed beings. Sons of the earth, let's stand together, children of humus and clay, and shoulder to shoulder valiantly defend the fatherland. No one will come and take it away from us once our mission is finally accomplished. It's not our fault if those bloodsuckers and grave robbers go and kill their children for the sole reason of blaming us after the fact. For if the deities of Mother Earth left our plains and our valleys and sought refuge on the peaks of volcanoes, that's because of a well-founded fear of the noise and the dust of their profane hoofs, and because they found peace in the haze above the craters. No one ever says that: I'm the only one in this country to occasionally whisper it.

The representatives of the international community, now everywhere you turn, will, as always, send us their list of grievances. Too bad for those ruminants with that confused look on their faces. . . . Thank goodness for us, the vast majority are with us and for us. If by some misfortune a single infant is spared, the Byumba forest will never forgive us. Better even, she'll demand that we demonstrate our seriousness and constancy, and more often than not will obtain these by severing the bloody cord that connects us to her. Pay heed to the sacred forest's soul and to its thousands of wandering spirits that expect blood to be spilled abundantly in their name. I have seen their eyes popping out in amazement, their herds with deep lacerations like cliffs. I know from magical science that these thousands and thousands of souls are thirsty and, what is more,

impatient. And not merely for blood: the whole body must be
sacrificed in order to assuage the daily thunder of the forest.
Each and every grove of trees, forest clearing, each dale and
each marsh will expect its share of flesh, and don't neglect in
your youthful zest the bamboos, the streams, the springs, and
the fumaroles. Our rights, under what are our banana trees,
must be restored. People of the clay, for far too long you have
been trampled, plundered, and humiliated, it is high time you
hold your head up and put your shoulders proudly back. The
spirits in the sacred forest are eagerly waiting for this, and I'm
not even mentioning all our comrades in the south, to the west
and east, who are chomping at the bit to pitch in and lend their
strong fraternal support once you get the ball rolling. Children
of the cultivators, let's exterminate the vermin. Let's chop off as
many heads as possible. We'll bring death to them, I swear, before death itself. We'll be like those hyenas in the savanna that
can sense the illness of other animals in the area and patiently
wait for a whole season to pass before reveling in a carcass when
the time comes. I can see in your eyes the glowing embers of
anger you have been suppressing for so long. You need to know
when to pull a rotten tooth before it contaminates the rest of the
mouth. Hold back for your own pleasure the rain fallen from
the heavens, and when you have had enough to drink, let the
rain overflow into the mass graves already filled with stiffened
bodies. Work the crowd into a frenzy with whistles, bells, and
drums. Let the conch shell horns sound the liberation.

The huts will be easy to set fire to, we know that from experience. Scour the countryside, and as always, the dogs, carrion,
and the rodents in the marshes will be our best allies. Rumors
will also greatly assist us. Whenever you speak in public, do
so under the protective mantle of our forefathers, in the wake
of the inspirational words of our great poets, sheltered under
the umbrella of our former and current leaders, such presti-

gious figureheads as Grégoire Kayibanda, "Father of the Nation" and of the social revolution, and the most holy Juvénal Habyarimana.

They succeeded in belittling us, in instilling a feeling of inferiority in us. They kept us in this state for centuries. Foreigners, all-conquering and proud, our daughters and hospitality weren't enough for them, they had to make us tenant farmers, indentured servants, subjugated. Our rebellions and acts of valor, engulfed, forgotten; our heroes, buried, decapitated; our history, falsified, distorted, dismantled and rewritten with the help of the foreign devils. Our youth have been degraded and thrown to the dogs. They've taken our language, our gods, and gone so far as to imitate our funerary rites. Abracadabra, that's all there is to it; now we're brothers, but always their subordinate. Well, there you are, that's some kind of machination! Innocently, some of us believe in the fable of hereditary fraternity contained in the dictum "Three ethnic groups, woven into one braid"—at best a lie, at worse deviltry. Well, since we're all soul brothers, then make sure you treat them as such, and don't think twice when it comes to splitting any fraternal heads in half with your machetes should your paths cross. One might well say that hereafter the Batutsi are an extinct race just like the aboriginals or the ancient peoples in the Old Testament. No Christian miracle will be capable of resurrecting them if we perform our job in the proper way. Enough with servitude, the whip, deprivation and debasement. We'll come down on them like a plague of locusts. With one cockroach for every eight or nine of us, no, what am I thinking, for every twelve of us, the harvest should take only a few days, wouldn't you say? As the old saying goes, "A cockroach will never become a butterfly." Once completely cleansed, Rwanda will once again be pure and virginal as in the early days of creation. Hills of bones will remain to burn slowly, and our agronomists are convinced these will produce the very best fertilizer. We are going to build the continent's tallest pile of corpses, which I'm really thrilled about, and this will elicit the admiration of connoisseurs. And now, come on, my children, raise your machetes and let's get to work!

AND THE DOGS FEASTED

Plump stray dogs with fat neck rolls have been feasting on dead bodies for weeks now. It's best to stay away from them, which is easier said than done when you can barely take more than a few steps without stumbling given the poor state of your Achilles' tendons that somehow miraculously didn't rupture under the blows of machetes.

Teats bursting, following the trail, the bitches have nothing of their former canine grace. Carrying diseases, rummaging through the forest, body snatchers, fighting over remains with other scavengers. Packs roaming from one site of carnage to another, between wells, from one marsh to the next. Columns of mad dogs blocking the hilltops right at daybreak, with shadowy and bloody muzzles. Voracious. Coyotes, guard dogs, the Lycaon pictus, jackals, all wretched depopulators of the same ilk.

Wild donkeys and lunatics riding all over the deserted hills, braying away in the emptiness at a day's journey from any normal setting. The dogs carry it with them in their genes, and the rivers of blood have awakened their pack mentality. From that point forward, the law of the pack prevails. Inebriated from the epidemic of decomposing corpses, the ferocious beasts feasted to their hearts' content. Intrepid lookouts, the birds of prey waited for the rains or for there to be a lull to clean up. Then came a plague of locusts. Swollen rivers filled with bloated corpses, dark and reddened wood, most likely stiff, cloud the marshes and suspend all movement. The heavens drum the final cadenza; nonstop flashes of light, thunderbolts and lightning. Later there were rounds of shelling, then all fell silent again, followed by more shelling.

What good would screaming do? In any case, who would hear you, come to your rescue? From the hills, bellicose clamors, unidentified braying and bleating, rent the silence. Best to retain some shred of dignity and remain deadly quiet. Only the land of the dead and the land of dreams rub shoulders; that of the living is far, far away.

Over in the corner, a woman of a certain age, alone, looks on attentively, quietly and respectfully. Her clothes are those afforded her social rank (very poor) and suitable for her age (advanced): a piece of loincloth fastened around the waist, an ochre dress put on over the head, barefoot.

"My name is Marie-Immaculée, I'm an old lady now, all by myself; all ten members of my family were exterminated. For weeks they thought I was also dead but, as you can see for yourself, Providence decided otherwise. Life does what it pleases. I don't have any tears left to shed. I don't have the strength to fight anymore. Those of us who survived are criticized. Whenever we go to the mayor or the authorities to ask for a bit of help, they look you up and down and stare at you condescendingly. You can go ahead and print that—I'm not afraid of anyone anymore."

"Please, tell me more."

"Everyone wonders why I hold on to this big old dog. He used to be skinny, but he fattened up on human flesh during the genocide. Folks say he even ate some of my family members. We all know each other around here and so he probably did eat people he knew. Some folks were only injured but the dogs finished them off and sent them to the afterlife. (Silence). As if they were helping the *Interahamwe* do their work."

"Why did you decide to keep him?"

"With me, you mean? Because he came back to me one day. I'm not sure how he escaped death. The young soldiers killed all the dogs that were eating the dead bodies. Now I call him Minuar in memory of the French name given to the UN peacekeeping mission that failed to protect us, not even the old ladies and children, even though they were well armed and could see all that was going on around here. So I call him Minuar. I can't even remember his old name."

A journey without stopovers to the furthest depths of inhumanity. The fertile udders of hatred and the trellis of the sky. As cold as marble or bare stone. A delicate skin. A deeply shaken world. The blood supplies have been used up, are now exhausted. Tired words, chewed a thousand times over. People kill for fun, just for the sake of it. On top of a building, in a humid valley, under an unmade bed. The victim is always raped first, just for a laugh, for nothing. At other times, because the clean shirt a cockroach is wearing made someone envious, or out of jealousy because his girl is taller than yours and because his brother lives abroad, suspicion reigned; no need to go searching for motives. Who will be left to save them if the other cockroaches are kept at a respectable distance from Mount Jali? A journey without stopovers to the depths of inhumanity.

The bereaved look in these eyes that have shed all their tears remains steadfast. A nation of vampires, sealed by a blood pact. A people who lost their icons, totems, and old books forever. Some victims carry with them such an acute fear of their neighbors that they would jump at the opportunity to enter the interstellar void. As soon as journalists or health-care workers ask you how you're doing, you feel deep inside you the absurdity of the question. All that remains of these exterminated families are hints of a skeleton in what is left of a peasant dress, a jaw or the fragment of a skull—by no means enough to ignite the spark that lies in each of us. Only the stench of gangrenous death lingers. Too weak to face the ashes at dawn. No sign of repentance on the horizon. A commodity nowhere to be found in this wasteland: trust in oneself and in others. Here, life as it was once has vanished. Joy is also stillborn. Well-meaning men and women, the most compassionate and the most inspiring, but also the most fragile, were the first to be killed. As happy as God in Rwanda. Not an ounce of sympathy. Only the unmitigated piety of the faceless survivors. No room for heroes. Only a few gravestones. More often an open hole in the ground in which the dome of a skull welcomes the onlooker's eye. Nothing has been done yet to dredge the hearts, to generate the momentum for a desirable and desired reconciliation.

Portrait of an Adolescent Militiaman

White blood-stained bandana that looks like the Japanese flag, perfectly centered and tightly wrapped around his head. Standing in a slick of blood, a machete in one hand, dispensing death in thousands of small denominations, running at full capacity for such a young age. A second machete hangs from his belt. He's smoking weed, guzzling, barking obscenities.

STORIES

NO, KIGALI IS NOT SAD

July 1998. Kigali. As a native of Djibouti and the arid lowlands of the Horn of Africa overlooked by the Ethiopian highlands, paradise for me has always been enveloped in the kind of luxuriant greenery found on Mount Kigali, which ended up, moreover, being the last bastion during the battle of that name; the aim had been to capture the large town named as the new capital by the grace of rural exodus. Only recently, in the mid-seventies, at the height of the social revolution, did it acquire, thanks to foreign aid, the minimum of decorum expected of political capitals. However, the southern university city of Butare (formerly named Astrid in honor of a Belgian queen), rather sleepy these days, has always harbored an unhealthy jealousy toward Kigali.

In this area where the soil can be earthy, cindery, or rich in silt, at times dusty or with lateritic ores as in Nyamirambo, the eucalyptus trees, reputed for depleting the groundwater, are parrot green. Lazy afternoons under amber skies. There has been no rainfall for months and folks are finding reasons for concern: Might the God of the Christians be definitively angry because of all that happened? But climate has nothing to do with the hot, dry khamsin winds of the Red Sea. I do my best to comfort my interlocutors by arguing that at least when it comes to the weather, hell is a long way from Rwanda. The grove of trees, hills, the scenery in general, are more of a foretaste of what paradise is like. Nonetheless, by digging a little into the past, one discovers that no less than six famines have struck the country during the twentieth century, which is not trivial for such a heavenly place. This enchantment might very well explain the immediate love felt by the missionaries when they arrived during the nineteenth century. A somewhat zany poet once told me that you cannot survive merely from contemplating the land, as beautiful and magical as it may be. This paradox is contained in the following phrase: "A land of Cockaigne!"

On the bus racing down the seven hills of the city, with me on board, I listen to the other passengers chatting away, to the rising and falling tones and linguistic subtleties, their glances full of tenderness and their eyes bright with excitement. If the word *ariko* is used over and over again, then that's because the discussion, just like the bus itself, is bumping along in jolts and jerks. It may not at first seem obvious, but this is just a little grain of sand in an otherwise well-oiled social machine. At the destination and before parting ways, after catching up after God only knows how long, chest to chest, hand in hand, warm embraces are exchanged.

Managed efficiently and with considerable tact by Spéciose, out of exile and back from Haiti, the La Mise Hotel, where we're staying a few more nights, is located in Nyamirambo, one of the livelier densely populated, poorer neighborhoods and commercial districts that is also home to Muslim Rwandans. To get from the Al Fatah Grand Mosque to the regional stadium, you have to take a bus that stops in front of the Petro-Rwanda gas station or the small Seventh-day Adventist church.

July 12, 1998. France has just won the World Cup. This is an incredible moment for all the children of the tricolor fatherland. But here, the reaction is quite different. Rwandans aren't feeling festive, all the more so given how the French army and political establishment repeatedly disgraced themselves prior to and after the genocide. I halfheartedly cheered for *les Bleus*, not so much for the way they played but rather because of the disappointing mediocrity of their Brazilian opponent. One or two car horns can be heard outside on account of a few nostalgic memories of the Franco-Rwandan friendship in evidence between François Mitterrand and Juvénal Habyarimana at the Franco-African summit held in 1990.

The sons and daughters of this country are working tirelessly to rebuild it. In every office you step into there's a civil servant eager to assist you, which is unfortunately a rare occurrence in most of the continent's administrative buildings. Better even, those who acquired skills abroad during the years of the ordeal and of exile are increasingly contributing to different sectors of society. Journalists in the morning, consultants for international organizations during the afternoon, teachers in the evening, juridical counselors on the weekends, while also lending a hand in a few other ways as well. In postgenocide Rwanda, no one expects special credit for these activities. Quite the contrary, this is the new norm and the elite (as well as the masses) no longer count their time, even if they do find time when duty calls to throw back a few cold Primus or Mützig beers before getting back to work the next day. The waiters and the waitresses are a bad influence, keeping a watchful eye on your glass and topping it off as soon as the level drops. This combination of business acumen and remnants of an ingrained tradition of hospitality and welcome that has been handed down over the years can prove a little unsettling for the newcomer ignorant of local customs and habits and, as is common in such instances, often clumsy in his words and gestures.

The buildings in Kigali's city center are home to numerous private dispensaries, medical offices, hair salons, pharmacies, and newly opened businesses. There is also a flourishing private security industry, a strong indication of the emergence of an active middle class, or at least the consequence of the widespread insecurity that resulted from years of criminal governance. Still, what is missing are bookshops. The Maison de la Presse doesn't really qualify, and so Librairie Caricas is the only establishment worthy of the name. There's also barely any music on the streets, with the exception perhaps of the voice of Annonciata Mutamuliza.

The scent of blood has vanished. The signs of the battle have disappeared, except for a few isolated buildings like the National Assembly. Life has been back to normal for quite some time now. The city is buzzing with activity, and there just isn't enough room for all this energy and these fresh ideas. The spaces I got to visit were too confined in relation to the enthusiasm and dynamism of the occupants. Courage increased with each passing day. One refrains from awakening the still waters of memory, sheathing wounded hearts in leather. One starts to miss a few vacation days here and there, neglect Sunday rest, forget a friend's wedding on the weekend, and stop getting the right amount of sleep. Unrestrained, we perform the task we've assigned ourselves.

RETURN TO KIGALI

A person is an individual humanity. Every man is a race.

MIA COUTO, MOZAMBICAN NOVELIST

To be vulnerable is to be fully human. It's the
only way you can bleed into other people.

ANTJIE KROG, SOUTH AFRICAN POET

On this nineteenth day of July 1999, I'm getting ready for a twenty-four-hour journey, Paris–Brussels–Nairobi–Kigali. The Sabena Airlines flight to Brussels is stormed by a group of thirty or so Guinean migrants, with bulky baggage and a horde of kids within easy reach. African immigrant families in Europe are recognizable from a distance, in every airport, because of the way they huddle around the check-in counter, by the way they are berated by the airline employees, and in their polite silence in the face of the insults they are subjected to. At times they can be overly eager in the way in which they follow instructions, the heads of households calling their spouses, offspring, cousins, and any other travel companions to order.

"South Africa is our dream, Rwanda our nightmare. . . . Everyone is worried about the gorillas in Rwanda. . . . But we are talking here today about a human decimation. To talk about an endangered species is to talk about the Tutsis in Rwanda today." This statement, made by Wole Soyinka, was republished in the progressive Spanish newspaper *El Pais* on May 23, 1994, at the height of the genocide and is, as far as I know, the first made on the subject by an African intellectual. This helps put into context the deafening silence of those bearded, bespectacled types and, more generally, of the continent's intellectuals. Speaking out in this manner demonstrates, if this were ever necessary, the extent to which Wole Soyinka is an unstoppable author, seasoned in the techniques of direct confrontation and attentive to the worldwide proliferation of misery. Having said this, his intervention in no way absolves all the other opinion makers for the absence of their reactions.

In Nairobi, the skyscrapers and high-tech buildings that make up the *downtown* area, so impressive at first sight for all those who have never left the sprawling shantytowns and dusty burgs of the Sahel, hide greater moral and social misery. From instinct, I can now better grasp the sociological realism found in the works of the Kenyan novelist Meja Mwangi, somewhat in the tradition of his illustrious compatriot Ngũgĩ wa Thiong'o, who remains a pariah for the authoritarian regime of Daniel Arap Moi.

When the day's over and as evening begins to fall, the crowded *matatu* (minibuses) unload their human cargo on the outskirts of town. Men in gray or blue-flame suits, the embodiment of the private protection and security companies cropping up all over the continent, from Cairo to the Cape and Dakar to Djibouti, share the main thoroughfares in the city center with the revelers, marauders, and prostitutes.

The flight between Nairobi and Kigali went smoothly aboard a small aircraft operated by Alliance Express, a marvel of economy and efficiency owned by a South African and Rwandan corporation, with South African pilots, easily recognizable because of their white skin and rocky accents, and an English- and French-speaking crew, which is worth mentioning since it serves to counter the persistent phantasms of certain voices of official francophonie for whom anglophone influence is everywhere, a phenomenon that historians once referred to as the Fashoda syndrome. Observing how this airline seamlessly connects, three times a week, the cities of Nairobi and Kigali, sometimes making stops in Entebbe, and given all the inconvenience I recently experienced with Sabena Airlines, I seize the opportunity to hoist the mainsail of Pan-Africanism. What if the African Renaissance promised by President Thabo Mbeki and so heartily desired by the vital forces of the continent were starting to materialize with actions of this kind?

Today, July 20, 1999, is my birthday. I've just turned thirty-four, an old man based on the norms in Rwanda after the genocide. Thankfully, no sign of gray hairs just yet. I've just landed in Kigali, where making your way through customs is pretty straightforward, comforting in fact, and definitely a pleasant change when compared to the harassment one experiences in Western European airports or the nonchalance and corruption in most African republics. Gratien, a Rwandan friend, who's in charge of logistics for our project, has come to pick me up. On the way from the airport he makes a slight detour via the Ministry of Youth and Sports, which is set up in the wings of the really big Amahoro Stadium—a word that symbolizes the most sought-after commodity in the land: peace—so that we can give his wife, Dany, a ride over to the Université Libre de Kigali, where she is taking night classes. For a long time, access to education was restricted to one group, which explains the sudden growth in schools and colleges in the country beyond the private ULK, an affinity that deliberately reminds us of the connection with a prestigious institution in Brussels. The will of the people of Rwanda to achieve success via education can be easily explained in terms of the highly selective pyramid-like system that is common throughout Africa, not forgetting the years of exile imposed on parents and the quota that, under the previous two regimes, categorically blocked access to those children born in the wrong families. The system responsible for the frustrations of yesteryear has culminated in an unquenchable thirst for knowledge—as good a way as any to turn things around: the urgency of life always prevails.

History in these parts is a barrel of dynamite, used abusively, and where only a fine line exists between overt falsification and minimum objectivity. However, deeply entrenched hatred between Tutsis and Hutus did not really exist prior to 1959, and

was never a recurrent theme in Rwandan history. Neverthe-
less, a few decades earlier, missionaries had succeeded with
their pernicious teachings in irrevocably damaging ancestral
religious beliefs and in altering both the temporal and eternal
balance of power.

Shifting power dynamics in which events that have previously been trivial can suddenly, because of a clumsy gesture, a
dispute over property, or the return of a swirling wind after a
spell of good weather, take a tragic turn in the blink of an eye.

The seven thousand prisoners held in Rilima prison are all
génocidaires ("those who commit genocide"), as classified in the
four separate categories recognized by the International Criminal Tribunal for Rwanda in Arusha, from the perpetrators to
the organizers and planners themselves, appear rather normal.
They engage in a variety of activities that couldn't be more human, such as weeding, exercising, or cooking. Sometimes they
dance; they pray a lot, but always in an orderly fashion. They
toe the line and the guards don't have to raise their voices to be
obeyed. This is a fairly unusual environment, strangely calm,
which someplace else could have disintegrated into a popular
uprising or driven individuals to desperate acts. Suicides are
relatively common among the jailers, some of whom come from
the ranks of the Patriotic Front, but are a rare occurrence in the
general prison population. There are few repentant offenders,
many distraught farmers, enclosed within a rigid hierarchy that
is as self-evident as it is highly effective.

Along with the Ivorian writer Véronique Tadjo, a Rwandan
interpreter, and the Dutch head of Penal Reform International,
an international NGO that monitors prison conditions and op-
erates in thirteen of the country's nineteen prisons—which is
not without its challenges given the sheer number of detainees
and their somewhat unusual status—I was able to gain access

without too much difficulty to the area reserved for inmates sentenced to death. We were welcomed with considerable passion, but always in an orderly manner; our presence disrupts the daily routine since visitors are rare. The people we met were determined, assured in their position, and didn't sound the slightest bit penitent. On the contrary, we found them to be accusatory and punctilious in the way that American attorneys can be, counterattacking each point we made, and with arguments that were a long way from the official rhetoric that of late has been marinating in notions of reconciliation and national harmony.

Once again, I find myself looking to the past and to the survivors of the Holocaust to find an explanation or at least something close to one.

> The diligent executors of inhuman orders, were
> not born torturers, were not (with few exceptions)
> monsters: they were ordinary men. . . . More dangerous
> are the common men, the functionaries ready to
> believe and to act without asking questions.
>
> PRIMO LEVI

You can learn a lot about a country from its newspapers. I just read in the June 26, 1999, edition of the *New Times*, the main English-language newspaper, a glaring exception in this country that the fanatics of francophonie have no reservations about describing as anglophile, namely that a delegation of Rwandan women attending a trade fair in Dar es Salaam were attempting to sell skeletal remains as souvenirs. A Tanzanian newspaper, the *Daily Mail*, broke the story. One of the women cited, a well-known businesswoman from Kigali, responded energetically, claiming that the whole story had been fabricated in Dar es Salaam by the Hutu refugee community and was aimed at sullying the reputation of the merchants attending the fair and of Rwandans in general. She also claimed a group of boisterous young rwandophones came up to her stand and starting asking, somewhat defiantly: "Why don't you just go ahead and sell skulls and bones while you're at it—you have an abundance of them in Rwanda—instead of all these handicrafts?" The height of cynicism or a heavy-handed provocation?

A real bookshop worthy of the name has just opened in Kigali a few streets from the main market and its pandemonium of wares, thereby dethroning the Catholic Librairie Caritas of its precarious reign. Ikerezi, since that is the shop's name, is run by a smiling Dutchman—one of these formidable Batavians settled in these lands of misfortune for decades—married to a Rwandan who died recently following an illness, a father, who gives of himself tirelessly. His co-workers should be very proud, because Ikerezi has everything a decent bookshop should have (recent newspapers and periodicals, books, school supplies, and even a good selection of CD-ROMs). *Rue de la récolte,* or Harvest Street—now isn't that a great name for a dispensary specializing in the fruits of the earth? A veritable beehive of activity right in the heart of the city, a rallying point for book lovers. A ray of hope in the sky above Kigali, welcome respite from the risks and hazards in force in the region.

The organization for survivors of the genocide, IBUKA, plans to publish a nominal dictionary in which all the names of victims of the genocide will be logged, beginning with the Kibuye Prefecture, a neighborhood as murderous as any other in a country in which death was measured by the million. In addition to the family name, given name, occupation, sex, and the place and date of death, data will also be gathered on the cause of death and the weapon used to kill.

"There are too many projects in the works," complains one Rwandan civil servant working to provide moral and material reparation to survivors, "too many NGOs, abbreviations and acronyms, press releases, too many residences protected by black security guards, too many humanitarian activities, too many experts on the ground, too many economic issues, too much money at stake, too many feel-good projects, too many locals to find jobs for, too many ageing white priests, too much official ranting, and can you believe it, even Kofi Annan claims to be truly sorry, too many niceties, too much complicity and hypocrisy on our side, too many needless utterances. . . . I apologize, but I am just being honest."

The Ethiopian soldiers were among the rare soldiers of MINUAR (UNAMIR, the United Nations Assistance Mission for Rwanda) to make their way into the hills and provide meaningful support right after the genocide. Birds continued to behave normally and glide over the hills, but the scavenging birds of prey could be spotted hovering determinedly. Oh, all those damaged minds, extinct lineages, family lines that have come to an end, these youth sandwiched between a rock and a hard place that will never know the secrets of love!

The sun breaks through for a few moments in an otherwise ominous sky, in which large dark clouds trudge along in a macabre procession. An oasis in a desert of inhumanity: apparently, the inhabitants of the predominantly Muslim neighborhoods—there's a small swahiliphone community that came from the coast and settled here, in the heart of Africa—in

places such as Nyamirambo in Kigali or Buyenzi in Bujumbura, demonstrated great moral courage by refraining, on the
one hand, from taking part in the massacre, and on the other
by sheltering as best they could people who had come running
into their district. They're a close-knit community, albeit a minority representing less than ten percent of the population in
this vast necropolis, and behave as if their religious affiliation
is more important than their ethnicity, which is certainly unusual in Rwanda and in neighboring Burundi, where the latter
provides the determining anthropological link and interpretive
grid.

One of my friends, the only Christian in a large Muslim family, admits that he's always the last person to be consulted when
it comes to family matters, long after the other members, Hutus
and Tutsis alike, have entered into conclave.

Before leaving, I was especially happy I got to meet up with
the good Dr. Rufuku in some hole in the wall in Nyamirambo,
all the more so because our meeting took place on my last afternoon in Kigali and because I was on the verge of missing him
altogether. After a great many hugs and lively introductions to
his circle of friends, he handed me a bottle of Primus and welcomed me with a "Clément-Robert, he's lost it," in reference to
a truculent and strange friend who had recently been misplaced
somewhere in the tortuous labyrinth of his past. Dr. Rufuku
hasn't changed much, he's just as active as he always was with
his group friends, relieving the ravages of the body and the
mind. He still hasn't lost the American accent that continues to
inflect his spoken French, which is for all intents and purposes
irreproachable, and he still claims to be forty-five years old for
the simple reason that he has stopped counting the years since
he returned from exile.

BUJUMBURA BEACH

I'm staring at the driver's neck in the taxi taking me from the airport to the center of Bujumbura. You can't really avoid looking at it at some point during the ride, especially when you're sitting in the backseat right behind him. Suddenly I notice two slashes, the one horizontal at the nape of the neck and the other vertical, running down the side of his skull. My senses are aroused before I have even set foot in the capital.

Although this is my first time in this airport, there's something familiar about it. I've felt like this on numerous occasions previously when arriving in the airport of an African capital I'm about to discover. Similar fragrances mixed in with the warm air and dust, the same indolent welcome at customs, and sometimes even the tropical architecture intermingled with oriental influences. With the time it takes to get from the plane to the terminal, you can literally take the temperature. This is something you can no longer do in ultramodern airports where you go straight from the antrum of the Boeing jet or Airbus to waiting in line to clear customs without so much as seeing the color of the sky or feeling the cold of day.

Bujumbura International Airport, as futuristic as it may appear from the outside, is more like a ghost ship in terms of activity since economic sanctions were slapped on the country by the international community after yet another military coup returned Pierre Buyoya, the former head of state, to the seat of power. Only a few regional airline planes can be seen sitting out on the runway, the small aircraft operated by some Air Baraka, of undetermined nationality. Not the slightest sign of any international fleet, even though Bujumbura is only six hours or so away by jet from Paris or Brussels. No comparison whatsoever with the bustling Jomo Kenyatta International Airport or the smaller but still very busy Grégoire Kayibanda International Airport in Kanombe, Kigali. In passing, it is worth noting how the first generation of independent African leaders sought to leave behind lasting reminders of their time in office by inscribing their names into the scenery, almost as if they weren't quite convinced by the vigor of their deeds.

Bujumbura is located on a vast incised plain, surrounded by wooded hills, and a light breeze blows over the undulating savanna grasslands. There are also countless plants, trees, and flowers that my Sahelian eyes and language cannot recognize and are incapable of naming. No sooner had I arrived than I was taken to the beach where all of Bujumbura's young and hip crowd hangs out on weekends. In other circumstances I might have thought this was a somewhat funny place to get a grasp of the country's realities. The term *beach* also has a strange ring to it when you use it right in the very heart of Africa, but this would be to forget all too easily that the lakes in the area are in fact ocean-like bodies of water. The port of Bujumbura, tucked away in a cove at the northeastern tip, is still the main port on Lake Tanganyika and sits across from the city of Uvira in what was not that long ago Mobutu's Zaire.

"So how are things at Cocktail Beach?" folks inquire in Kigali, as a way of asking what life is like on the other side of the border in Burundi, where a large number of Rwanda's population today once lived in exile in what was at one time the biggest and oldest refugee community on the continent. This is also a way of forgetting for just a few minutes the challenges of everyday life or, in a more subtle way, to summon the more relaxed way of living before the genocide. And with good reason, for it is three times more expensive to live in Paul Kagame's Rwanda than it is in Burundi.

The small stretch of beach known as Cocktail or Malibu Beach, just over two miles long, is quite remarkable. Affluent youth gather here in the early afternoon until sundown, the children of military leaders who have been taking turns holding the reins of power without interruption since army captain Michel Micombero overthrew the monarchy in 1966, with the exception of a short-lived and bloodstained truce during the presidency of the late Melchior Ndadaye and his first democratically elected government—a man who, along with Prince Rwagasore, now stands as the country's other martyr. The cover charge is 500FB (Burundi francs, roughly one American dollar), a way of sorting the wheat from the chaff. You can tell the customers are well fed, their look in tune with today's so-called modern times: baggy pants sagging below the waistline, Nike high-top sneakers, stylized sunglasses, and NBA basketball player jerseys. American-sounding names (Billy, Eddy, Nancy) are shouted out, followed with bursts of wild, juvenile laughter. Jimmy and Freddy whistle their approval at the sight of a sister's breasts, an especially carnal girl whose powers are such that she can easily awaken those obscure desires buried in each and every one of us. One's gait sets the tone, and you don't strike up a friendship with just anybody. This is a select club, and you can't just waltz in. Their dreams aren't that different from those of the jet set the world over, from Durban to Algiers, New Delhi and Detroit, or in Nairobi or Recife, but for their fellow countrymen stuck in the interior, from Muyinga to Mabanda, or right in the middle of the country in Gitega, these would be considered exotic.

The effects of the current economic downturn are obvious. The Saint-Paul bookshop, the only one in the capital, is sparsely stocked. A couple of shelves, fig leaves, barely anything on the situation in Burundi as opposed to Rwanda, for which there is both considerable recent interest and concern. It's clear that Burundi is a country engaged in a war of attrition: a curfew has been in place since 1993 and the army only controls the capital and the immediate surrounding area. Several times in its short postcolonial history, namely in 1962, 1965, 1972, 1988, and 1993, to only mention those crises in which there was the most significant bloodshed, a military junta in the hands of a radical Tutsi general staff has taken part in what has been referred to euphemistically as "selective genocides," which have decimated civil society and the Hutu middle class, thereby triggering the mass exile and scattering of hundreds of thousands of inhabitants, a situation reminiscent of the Rwandan impasse that resulted in the genocide that is now known to all.

The two plates of the scale are equally afraid. On the outskirts of the city, folks wake up almost every morning to find new corpses littering the broken sidewalks. Locals learned some time ago to step over the bodies so that life could carry on—life somehow always finds a way to do so. The urgency of life, we are told. People seem to be enjoying the relative tranquility, and the city feels more like a deserted resort. Thrust into isolation and self-sufficiency by the international community, the country now draws, somewhat paradoxically, on its own resources and, with a helping hand from cross-border collusions, has tiptoed along on the brink of disaster much longer than expected.

One friend, a touch more forthcoming than most—laconism is, let's not forget, a national sport, and besides, it's never really a good idea in any dictatorship, whether tropical or other, to fully open one's heart up—was telling us how kids born after 1993 can't begin to imagine what life was like in Bujumbura before the curfew and the threat of assailants. In fact, neither can we. By contrast, Kigali has always been less inviting, less polished, ultimately more provincial—which is not really surprising given that Buja, as lovers like to call it, and they are plentiful in the subregion, was once the capital of the colonial territory of Ruanda-Urundi administered by the Belgians.

This partially holds true to this day: one need only consider how the young upper-crust crowd have managed to carve out this safe and liberating cocoon for themselves for a few hours every Saturday and Sunday afternoon on these few square feet of sand, congested with Japanese or, more likely even, South Korean SUVs, and closed to the public the rest of the week for obvious safety reasons. Security concerns remain an obsession shared by everyone in this small country marinating in ethnic hatred, the root cause of political violence since independence in 1962. "Security" is also the term that keeps cropping up in the multiparty talks being held in Arusha and facilitated by Julius Nyerere. Based on the stories one finds in the newspapers published up and down the Ntahangwa River, Burundians are still preoccupied with the Arusha Accords, a subject that continues to exacerbate tensions. The security concerns that were once on everyone's mind have wasted no time impregnating everyday interactions. For example, if a young man is a little too pushy and not respectful of the rules of good behavior, then the young woman will rebuke him by calling him an "assailant"—in other words, through recourse to the official term used by Tutsi soldiers to describe the Hutu rebels. In Rwanda, they were called the "infiltrators" before they were disposed of and hunted down into the remotest cadaverous depths of Zaire. Lately, the infiltrators aren't talked about much. They, too, have not yet spoken their last word.

Afterword

This book is part of the collective project "Rwanda: écrire par devoir de mémoire" (Rwanda: Writing by Duty of Memory), an initiative launched by the Fest'Africa Festival (Association for the Arts and Media of Africa). The Fondation de France also made this work possible thanks to the Initiatives d'artiste program, which supports artists wishing to tackle important societal issues.

Note on Translations

All translations of Aimé Césaire's work are from the following:

Aimé Césaire: The Collected Poetry. Translated by Clayton Eshleman and Annette Smith. Berkeley: University of California Press, 1983.

Aimé Césaire: Lyric and Dramatic Poetry, 1946–82. Translated by Clayton Eshleman and Annette Smith. Charlottesville: University Press of Virginia, 1990.

Aimé Césaire: Discourse on Colonialism. Translated by John Pinkham. New York: Monthly Review Press, 1972.

Other translations include the following:

Couto, Mia. *Every Man Is a Race.* Translated by David Brookshaw. Oxford: Heinemann Publishers, 1994.

Levi, Primo. *The Reawakening.* Translated by Stuart Woolf. New York: Touchstone, 1995.

Notes

Preface: Post-Genocide Rwanda

*This final section of the preface was written by Abdourahman Waberi fifteen years after the genocide and originally published as "Rwanda: The Flame of Hope," translated by Nicole Ball and David Ball. Translation © 2009 by Nicole Ball and David Ball. Published in the November 2009 issue of Words without Borders, http://www.wordswithoutborders.org/article/rwanda -the-flame-of-hope. By permission of Words without Borders (www.wordswithoutborders.org). All rights reserved.

1. A member since 1970, Rwanda left Les Instances de la Francophonie at the Francophonie Summit that took place in Quebec in 2008. English would henceforth be used in the Rwandan administration and in education. "We give priority to the English language which will make our children more competent and will help our vision for developing our country," said President Paul Kagame.

2. The report of the National Independent Commission, whose mission was to gather proof that the French government was implicated in the preparation and carrying out of the 1994 genocide, also called the Mucyo Commission Report after its

president, is available on the Internet and was made public in August 2008.

3. I wish to thank Catherine Coquio, professor of literature (University of Poitiers and Paris IV) and president of AIRCRIGE (International Association for Research on Crimes against Humanity and Genocides).

Fictions

1. Translator's note: After this book was first published, Father Wenceslas Munyeshyaka was charged with genocide and torture in the mass slaughter of Tutsis. His case has been reviewed in Rwanda, at the International Criminal Tribunal for Rwanda (ICTR), and in the French courts, which recently concluded: "From our investigations, it appears the role of Wenceslas Munyeshyaka during the 1994 genocide raised a lot of questions. But the probe was not able to formally corroborate specific acts pertaining to his active participation."

ABDOURAHMAN A. WABERI
is a novelist, essayist, poet, and short-story writer. Born
in Djibouti, he is Professor of French and Francophone
literature at George Washington University. The
author of *Transit, In the United States of Africa, Passage
of Tears,* and *La Divine Chanson,* he has been awarded
the Stefan-Georg-Preis, the Grand Prix Littéraire
d'Afrique noire, and the Prix biennal "Mandat pour
la liberté." He was named one of the "50 Writers of
the Future" by the French literary magazine *Lire.*

DOMINIC THOMAS
is Madeleine L. Letessier Professor of
French and Francophone Studies at the
University of California, Los Angeles.

Printed in the USA
CPSIA information can be obtained
at www.ICGtesting.com
LVHW040522010924
789807LV00006B/23